For Max & Nora; and to Kathleen, with gratitude
—Lori Alexander

For Annette, Ellie, Lewis & Joe
—Craig Cameron

ISBN 978-0-06-225015-5

The artist used a combination of pencil, watercolors,
and Photoshop to create the digital illustrations for this book.
Typography by Rachel Zegar
21 22 SCP 10 9 8 7 6
❖
First Edition

# BACKHOE JOE

Written by **Lori Alexander**   Illustrated by **Craig Cameron**

**HARPER**

*An Imprint of HarperCollinsPublishers*

Nolan was collecting a few rocks when he heard a growl. There, in the middle of the street, he saw a stray . . .

. . . backhoe.

Nolan took a step closer.
*Beep! Beep! Beep!*
The backhoe reversed into the bushes.

Nolan had *always* wanted a pet backhoe.

So he whistled.

He called, "Heeere, big fella!"

But the backhoe wouldn't budge.

The rocks in Nolan's backpack
gave him an idea.

The tasty treats were scooped up in no time.

Nolan gave the backhoe a pat behind the loader,
which made his bucket wiggle like crazy.

"I'll call you ... Joe."

"Look what followed me home," Nolan said.
"I'm going to keep him. He won't be a bother."
Joe buried his cone in the flower bed. Then he leaked all over the driveway.

"See?" Nolan said. "He likes it here."
Mom and Dad weren't so sure.
"This backhoe isn't trained," Mom said.
"I'm on it," Nolan replied.

He started with a few simple commands:

"Come!"

Joe revved at the mailman.

"Stay!"

Joe treaded through Mr. Oldman's grass.

"Leave it!"

Joe dug in the garbage.

Nolan soon realized the problem—Joe had too much energy.
*When I have too much energy, Dad asks me to play catch.*

But Joe lost all the balls.

When I have too much energy,
Mom takes me to the park.

But Joe hogged all the sand.

Nolan didn't know what to do. If he couldn't train Joe, Mom and Dad would never let him stay.

He kicked at a rusty old fence. The gate creaked open. Joe sped inside. Nolan had found the perfect place for Joe to dig.

Joe even helped Nolan with his rock collection.

When it was time to go, Nolan took a deep
breath and tried another command.

"Joe . . . home!"

This time, Joe listened.

*I did it! I did it! Joe is trained!*
Nolan and Joe coasted for home—together.

But halfway there, Joe put on the brakes.

"This isn't our house, Joe. Make a left at the next . . ."

That's when Nolan spotted the flyer.

"It can't be you! You're a different yellow."
Joe's bucket drooped.
Nolan stared at the picture. He stared at Joe.
They were a perfect match.

Lost Backhoe
Please Call!
Reward!

"Someone's missing you," Nolan whispered.
"And I think you miss them, too."

Nolan knew what he had to do.
When Joe's owner arrived, Nolan wondered
if he'd ever see his friend again.

Luckily, Nolan had earned himself a
generous reward: a new hat, an exciting trip,
and as many rocks as he could carry.

But the best part of all was visiting
Backhoe Joe at *his* house.

"Such a responsible thing you did," Nolan's parents said proudly. "We think you're ready for a pet of your very own."

Then Nolan remembered how much work Joe
was. "Maybe I should get something that won't dig.
Something that will sit still—and purr. How about . . ."

"A cement mixer!"